A Visit to the Doctor

This book is dedicated to Dr. Peter Czuczka

and all of the other amazing pediatricians

who work so hard to keep our kids healthy.

-SKL

ISBN: 978-1-60169-153-8

Published by innovativeKids®
A division of innovative USA®, Inc.
18 Ann Street
Norwalk, CT 06854
iKids is a registered trademark in Canada and Australia.
www.innovativekids.com

Printed in China
1 3 5 7 9 10 8 6 4 2

First Edition

Today is doctor day!

My doctor has known me since
I was a tiny baby.

He takes good care of me, and
he always makes me laugh!

Sometimes I visit the doctor when I'm sick. He knows just what to do to make me feel better.

Today I'm not sick. I have a
check-up. The doctor will check
that I'm growing big and strong.

I have lots of fun in the waiting
room. There are toys to discover,
games to play, and books to read.

Soon, the nurse calls my name. It is my turn to go in.

I sit up on the big table and get undressed.

The nurse weighs
me on the scale . . .

. . . and measures
how tall I am. Boy,
I've grown so much!

Then the doctor
comes in. He makes
me smile right away!

The doctor uses his stethoscope to listen to my heartbeat. It feels a little cold, but it doesn't hurt.

th-thump
th-thump

I get to listen, too. It sounds so cool!

Next, the doctor takes out his special light.

He uses it to look in my eyes,

in my nose, and in my ears.

He says he sees an elephant in there!

The doctor tells me to open my mouth and say ahhhhh.

"Ahhhhhh."

He uses a flat stick to hold down my tongue so that he can see my throat.

After that, the doctor taps my knee gently with a funny looking hammer.

My leg kicks up and almost hits him in the nose.

He says my reflexes are very good!

He puts a cloth wrap around my arm to check my blood pressure. It feels funny as it squeezes my arm.

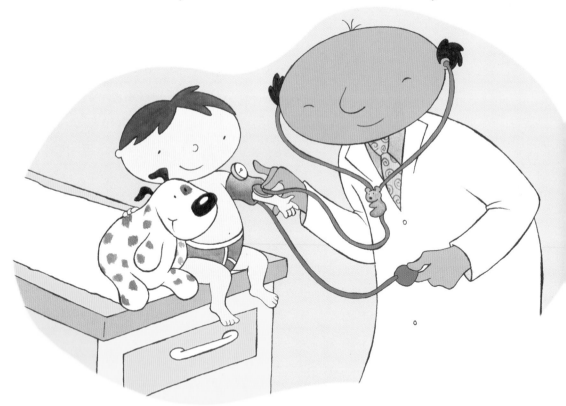

I ask him to do it again.

Then the doctor presses gently on
my tummy to feel what's inside.
He says he feels a hamburger and
an apple.

It sure
does tickle!

The nurse comes back in and says it's time for a shot. She gives one to my dog first. He doesn't seem to mind.

Now it's my turn.

She tells me that this shot is a
special kind of medicine that will
help me stay healthy.

I am very brave. I hold onto my
mom, and I only feel a pinch.

The doctor says
I had a great
check-up.

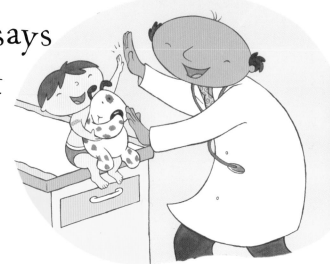

He lets me pick a special sticker.

Mom is proud of me. I am
happy, too.

I can't wait to get home and play!

Hooray for doctor day!

21

A Note to Parents

Visiting the doctor's office can be stressful for toddlers and young children. Role playing is a great way to help children know what to expect from their doctor visit. It is also a relaxing way to take away the fear and focus on the fun.

Here are some ideas to try before your doctor visit:

- Use a favorite stuffed animal to role play the doctor's exam with your child. Be sure to let your child be the doctor. This will give him or her a feeling of control and it may even get him or her excited about the upcoming doctor visit.

- Encourage your child to begin the doctor's exam on his or her stuffed animal or on you! Using a toy doctor's kit or other homemade props, tell your child what to do and let him or her do it.

- First, tell your child that the doctor will measure the patient's weight and height. Let your child measure the stuffed animal's height and then place it on the scale. You can even give him or her paper and a pencil to record the results.

- Next, use a toy stethoscope and tell your child to listen to the patient's chest and back. Have your child move the stethoscope around on the stuffed animal and make sounds for the heartbeat and for breathing in and out.

- Then, have your child use a toy or mini flashlight as an instrument to look into the stuffed animal's eyes, ears, and nose.

- A toy mallet or a small pencil with a rubber eraser can be used to gently tap on the knees of the stuffed animal.

- A sweat band can be used to wrap around the stuffed animal's arm to role play blood pressure.

- Then, show your child how the doctor will use his or her hands to press gently on the belly area. Have your child do this carefully on the stuffed animal.

- Now, give your child a popsicle stick so he or she can pretend to hold down the stuffed animal's tongue to get a good look in its throat.

- Finally, have your child use a toy syringe to give his or her stuffed animal a shot. Remind your child to tell his or her animal that it will only pinch for a second and that it will make sure he stays healthy and strong.

Remember to present the check-up as a positive experience.

Portray your doctor as a kind and friendly person who will help your child stay healthy so he or she can learn and play. Prepare your child for what will happen during the check-up. He or she will be more comfortable and cooperative when he or she knows and understands the purpose for the check-up.

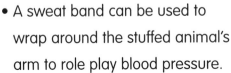

Your doctor helps keep you healthy from head to toe!
Can you find these parts on your body?

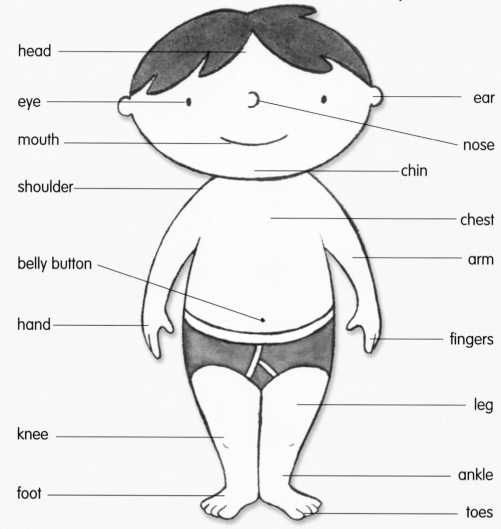

head

eye

mouth

shoulder

belly button

hand

knee

foot

ear

nose

chin

chest

arm

fingers

leg

ankle

toes